Praise for my other books

'Will make you laugh out loud, cringe and snigger, all at the same time'
–LoveReading4Kids

'Very funny and cheeky'
–Booktictac, Guardian Online Review

Waterstones Children's Book Prize Shortlistee!

'I LAUGHED SO MUCH, I THOUGHT THAT I WAS GOING TO BURST!'
Finbar, aged 9

'The review of the eight year old boy in our house...
"Can I keep it to give to a friend?"
Best recommendation you can get' – Observer

'HUGELY ENJOYABLE, SURREAL CHAOS'
–Guardian

I am still not a Loser
WINNER of
The Roald Dahl
FUNNY PRIZE
2013

EGMONT
We bring stories to life

First published in Great Britain 2015
by Egmont UK Ltd
The Yellow Building, 1 Nicholas Road, London W11 4AN

Text and illustration copyright © Jim Smith 2015
The moral rights of the author-illustrator have been asserted.

ISBN 978 1 4052 6803 5

barryloser.com
www.egmont.co.uk

A CIP catalogue record for this title is available from the British Library

Printed and bound in Great Britain by the CPI Group

69033/001

Barry Loser

and the case of the crumpled carton

Produced and directed by

Jim Smith

Worst name ever

My mum and dad are so busy looking after my brand new baby brother, Desmond Loser the Second, I sometimes wonder if they know I even exist.

pure evil

Like the other day, when my Granny Harumpadunk and her boyfriend Mr Hodgepodge came round to visit. My mum's favourite show, Detective Manksniff, was on TV, and I'd snuggled up to her on the comfy sofa, using her belly as a pillow.

Detective Manksniff

chewing on straw

Granny Harumpadunk and
Mr Hodgepodge were squidged on the
uncomfy sofa, squinting through their
matching glasses at the TV.

Granny

Hodge

'Ooh, now there's a good-looking
man,' warbled my granny as Detective
Manksniff stirred his cocktail with a
straw, and Mr Hodgepodge rolled his eyes.

'SHHH!' shushed my mum. 'I'm trying to enjoy my show,' she said, and I sniggled at her loserness, even though I was secretly quite enjoying it too.

'WAAAHHH!!!' screamed my dad from the downstairs bathroom, where he was changing Desmond Loser the Second's nappy for the nineteenth time that morning. 'DESMOND'S WEED IN MY FACE AGAIN!'

I heard my mum's belly do a gurgle and imagined myself curled up inside it, the same size as my annoying little brother.

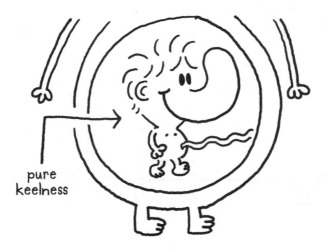

pure
keelness

'What was I like when I was a baby, Mum?' I said.

'I'm coming, Desmond!' cried my mum, comperleeterly ignoring my question, and she leaped off the sofa, wobbling down the hallway to help.

'Des-mond,' murmured Mr Hodgepodge, as if he'd only just heard it for the first time. 'What a terrific name for a little boy!' he smiled, and I wondered why everyone in my whole entire life had to have such loserish names, me included.

my autograph
(so you can't
read 'Loser') —

Barry

'Desmond Loser the First would've been proud!' beamed Granny Harumpadunk, heaving herself off the uncomfy sofa and doddering over to the mantelpiece, and she lifted up a photo of my Great Uncle Desmond, who was the biggest Loser that ever lived.

She put the picture back on the mantelpiece and picked up a little pig made out of china.

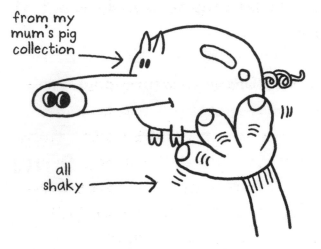

from my mum's pig collection →

all shaky →

'Do you think your mum wants this, Barry?' she said, and I shrugged, not listening at all, because Detective Manksniff had finished and MY favourite TV show, **Future Ratboy**, was on next.

'MAUREEN, DO YOU WANT THIS PIG OR CAN I SELL IT AT THE JUMBLE SALE?' screeched Granny Harumpadunk down the hallway to my mum, and I blew off into my sofa cushion out of shock.

That's all Granny Harumpadunk's been doing recently, collecting stuff for her boring old jumble sale, which is in Mogden Hall on Saturday from 10am till 3pm with a live magic show by The Great Hodgepodge and his glamorous assistant, Madame Harumpadunk, at 1pm sharp.

what it says on poster

'Sell it. She's got millions of them,' whispered my dad, tiptoeing into the lounge with Desmond Loser the Second asleep on his shoulder.

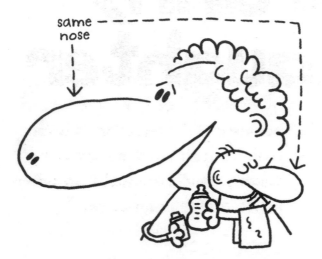

same nose

'Barry, turn that TV down,' he mouthed, and I was just about to press the mute button on the remote control, seeing as it was only the adverts, when I saw a carton of Tears of Granny Laughter pop up on the screen.

Tears of Granny Laughter

'Salute the keelness!' I shouted, leaping off the sofa and doing a quadruple-reverse-salute, which is what I do when my favourite advert comes on TV.

BOINNGGG!

Tears of Granny Laughter is this keel new drink they've started selling at Feeko's Supermarkets.

It comes in three granny flavours, Beryl, Irene and Gertrude, and the advert is all about how they make it.

It starts with Beryl, Irene and Gertrude queuing up to go into a cinema.

Then you see them laughing at a man in an old black-and-white film who's hanging off a building with his legs waggling everywhere.

The three grannies are all wearing massive 3D glasses that have been specially made to catch the tears of laughter zigzagging out of their eyes, and at the end of the film all the tear-juice is poured into cartons of Tears of Granny Laughter.

Beryl again

special glasses

tears

popcorn

carton

'Can I have some money for a Tears of Granny Laughter, Dad? Can I, Daddypoos? Can I? Can I Can I?' I said, running over and tugging my dad on his elbow, and Desmond Loser the Second opened his eyes and started screaming.

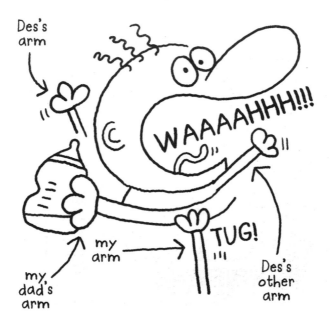

My mum wobbled back into the room, swinging a see-through plastic bag full of Desmond's poo. 'SHUSH, BARRY!' she whisper-shouted, stroking Desmond Loser the Second's cheek. 'You're upsetting Baby Des!'

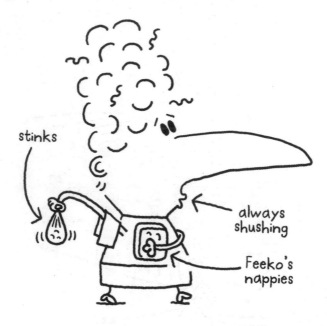

stinks

always shushing

Feeko's nappies

Granny Harumpadunk slipped the china pig into her handbag and shuffled over to look at the baby.

'Ooh, you're the loveliest thing since sliced bread, aren't you!' she cooed, and I wondered what was so amazing about sliced bread.

'Mu-um,' I squeaked in my babiest voice ever, seeing as that's what she seems to like so much these days, 'Dad said I could have some money for a Tears of Granny Laughter.'

'Tears of Granny Laughter,' murmured my mum, as if she'd heard the name somewhere before. 'Isn't that that terrible new drink Feeko's have been making out of little old ladies?'

'It's not real, that's just the advert!'
I groaned, because everyone knows
Feeko's doesn't use ACTUAL granny
tears to make Tears of Granny
Laughter. But my mum wasn't listening.

'I'm not having you drinking that stuff, Barry,' she said, taking Desmond off my dad and peering into his eyes the way I peer into my cuddly **Future Ratboy**'s.

lives in its box

Future Ratboy

"PLAY IT KEEL!"

I clenched my fists and felt a Tear of Barry Annoyance start to work its way out of my eyehole.

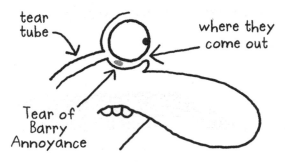

tear tube

where they come out

Tear of Barry Annoyance

'But Mu-um, everyone at school drinks it!' I wailed, which wasn't comperleeterly true. Only Anton Mildew in my class had tried Tears of Granny Laughter so far.

Anton Mildew

Anton Mildew is the editor of our school newspaper, The Daily Poo. Ever since he said that Tears of Granny Laughter was even tastier than Fronkle, all I've wanted to do is drink a carton.

'PLEE-EEASE!' I whined, but not in an annoying, whiney way.

'QUIET, BARRY!' said my mum, without even looking at me.

I stuck my tongue out at Desmond and was just about to storm up to my bedroom, when Mr Hodgepodge heaved himself off the sofa and plodded over to where I was standing.

He was wearing his sparkly bow tie, which he thinks makes him look like a magician.

'What's that in your ear, Barry?' he grinned, reaching out his shaky hand, and a 50p coin appeared between his fingers.

my ear

'You go enjoy your bottle of Grandma Pop!' he winked, dropping the 50p in my palm, and I slid it into my pocket before my mum and dad could see. Not that they were looking. Because they were too busy staring at Desmond Loser the Second.

Detective
Manksniff
straw

It was the next day and I was skateboarding down the road to catch up with my best friends, Bunky and Nancy.

actually going really slow

'Mornkeels, Barry!' said Bunky, as I skidded to a stop, trying to work out why he reminded me of Detective Manksniff all of a sudden. I looked him up and down and scratched my bum.

Bunky

'Hmmm, it's not your voice,' I said, thinking back to when Bunky had just said good morning to me. 'Detective Manksniff's voice is all deep and drawly. Yours sounds like a little old granny-dog's yap,' I smiled.

Bunky scrunched his face up, not really knowing what in the keelness I was going on about.

'It's not your hat either,' I mumbled. 'Detective Manksniff wears a keel detective hat, and you don't wear a hat at all,' I said, flicking Bunky's hair at the front, where it sticks up like a hand.

Nancy sighed, half bored, half wondering if I'd gone stark raving bonkers.

Nancy

'It definitely isn't your smile,' I frowned, poking my nose right up to Bunky's face. 'When Detective Manksniff smiles, you know he knows something you don't know,' I said. 'When YOU smile, you know you don't know anything AT ALL.'

KNOWS SOMETHING   DOESN'T

Bunky bonked me on the nose and I made a noise like a car horn. 'Thanks a lot, Barry!' he said, chewing on a straw.

me if I was a car

BEEP!

My eyebrows did a waggle. 'AH-HA,
it's that straw!' I said, pointing at the
straw, which was white with keel little
pink tear shapes dotted all over it.

'Whenever Detective Manksniff's
trying to solve one of his really hard
mysteries, he pulls the straw out of
his cocktail and starts chewing on it,'
I warbled. 'That's what's making you
look like him!'

straw

his
favourite
cocktail

Bunky smiled his smile he smiles when he doesn't really care about what I'm saying. Then he pointed the straw at me and blew.

PFFFT!

'OW-AH!' I screamed, as the tiniest rolled-up ball of paper in the whole wide world amen shot out of the straw and hit me on the ear lobe.

I snatched the straw off Bunky and
snapped it in half, which isn't easy,
seeing as straws are bendy, not snappy.

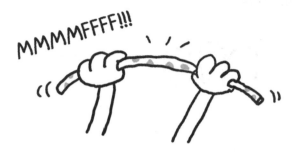

Bunky smiled, not in the keelest bit
bothered about me snapping his straw.
'Plenty more where that came from!'
he said, pointing at a poster for Tears
of Granny Laughter right next to
where we'd stopped.

'You-you've tried it?' I gasped,
suddenly realising where he'd got
the straw from.

'Eeve keelse!' smiled Bunky, which is how we've started saying 'of course', by the way. 'My sister bought me a carton of Gertrude flavour last night,' he said, and I wished I had an older sister who bought me cartons of Tears of Granny Laughter like Bunky, instead of a baby brother who stole my mum and dad.

Bunky's sister (Binky)

nose ring (not bogie)

'Wh-what's it taste like, Bunky?' I warbled, leaning against Nancy so I didn't fall over out of jealousy.

'Alright I spose . . . Not as nice as Fronkle,' he said, and he started waggling his legs around like the man in the Tears of Granny Laughter advert. 'That reminds me, I haven't weed it out yet . . .' he giggled.

Bunky's belly

Tears of Granny Laughter

My ears couldn't believe themselves. How could a drink made out of old grannies' tears not be the tastiest thing in the whole wide world amen?

'What are you, NUTS?' I said, which is what Detective Manksniff says when his ears can't believe THEMselves. 'Tears of Granny Laughter is the keelest thing since **Future Ratboy!**'

Nancy rolled her eyes, picking up Bunky's snapped-in-half straw and putting it in a bin.

CHUCK

'A lot of people don't like those adverts, you know,' she said, as three real-life grannies doddered past just like Beryl, Irene and Gertrude, except without the special glasses.

'Boo, naughty drink!' shouted the first granny, waggling her walking stick at the poster, and the second one shook her fist in the air.

'Ban Tears of Granny Laughter!' croaked granny number three as they wobbled off at two centimetres per hour.

'See!' smiled Nancy, and a shiver went down my spine. What if they DID ban my favourite drink before I even got to taste it? Since Desmond Loser the Second had come along and stolen my mum and dad off me, slurping on a carton of Tears of Granny Laughter was the only thing I had to live for.

'As if they'd ban the keelest drink since sliced keelness!' I said, not realising what was about to happen next.

Mayor Plunkett

'OUT OF THE WAY LOSEROIDS, THIS IS AN EMERGENCE-WEE!' screamed Bunky as we got to the school gates, and he zoomed across the playground towards the toilets.

WHOOSH!

waggling

Nancy chuckled to herself and picked up a copy of The Daily Poo from the stack next to the gates. 'Er, you might want to read this, Barry,' she said, suddenly not chuckling at all, so I picked one up too.

Daily Poo
↓

GASP!

'TEARS OF GRANNY LAUGHTER BANNED!' read my eyeballs, not believing themselves. 'Th-this must be a joke ...' I stuttered, and I went to lean on Nancy, but she'd walked off so I fell on the floor instead.

'Enjoy your trip, Barold?' sneered Gordon Smugly from my class, who's the sort of smug, ugly Gordon who's only happy when someone else like me is UNhappy.

SMUG
+UGLY
=SMUGLY

'It wasn't a trip, Gordon, it was a FALL,' I cried, and he chuckled to himself like one of the baddies in an episode of Detective Manksniff, except less scary.

'Yes, well, dreadful news about Tears of Granny Laughter, isn't it?' he drawled, and I squinted my eyes, wondering what he was up to. 'Hope you get yourself a carton before they all sell out . . .' he smiled, jangling a handful of coins inside his pocket.

From the sound of Gordon's jangle, he could afford to buy every carton in Mogden. And that's exackerly the sort of thing he'd do, just to ruin my life.

'Better get down to Feeko's sharpish after school, Barold!' he snortled, gliding off on his tiptoes, and I looked around for someone a bit less Gordonish to talk to.

Anton Mildew was slumped on a bench, Tears of Anton Sadness zigzagging down his cheeks. 'IT'S THE WORST DAY OF MY LIFE!' he wailed, and I crawled towards him, seeing as I was still lying on the floor from my fall-over from before, and getting up is BORING.

CRAWL

'It's all Mayor Plunkett's fault!'
snuffled Anton, blowing his nose on
his Daily Poo. 'She said the Tears of
Granny Laughter adverts were cruel to
grannies and ordered Feeko's to stop
selling it immedikeely.'

'Good riddance to it, that's what I say!'
burped Darren Darrenofski, slurping on
a can of Fronkle, which is his favourite
drink since sliced Darren. 'Tears of Granny
Laughter is for losers!' he chuckled.

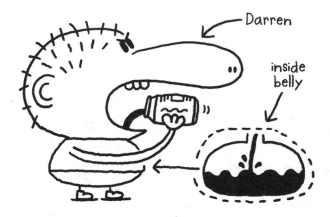

Darren

inside
belly

Anton crumpled his Daily Poo into a ball and threw it at Darren's head, just as Sharonella from our class stomped over, doing her angry face.

Shazza

STOMP!

STOMP!

Sharonella's been in a bad mood with Anton ever since he did a front page exclusive in The Daily Poo saying she might be the Phantom Air-Freshener Thief.

The Phantom Air-Freshener Thief is this mysterious person who's been going round all the toilets in Mogden School stealing the plug-in air-fresheners.

Feeko's air-freshener (looks like a nose)

the thief

smell comes out of nostrils

'Fanks a lot for saying I was the Phantom Air-Freshener Thief, Anton,' screeched Sharonella. 'As if I'd want to steal a stupid air-freshener!' she scoffed, her perfume wafting up my nostrils. 'I'll get you back for this, Mildew!' she screeched, stomping off again just as Bunky bounded over, zipping up his flies.

'What in the unkeelness is going on here?' he yapped, and I realised he hadn't heard the news.

'Get ready to not believe your ears,' I said, and I started to tell him everything that had just happened, which was pret-ty boring for everyone else, seeing as they already knew.

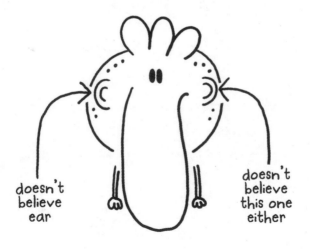

doesn't believe ear

doesn't believe this one either

Cardboard cut-out Irene

After that I had to sit through a whole day at school, while all the Feeko's in Mogden were selling out of Tears of Granny Laughter. Then it was home time, apart from the fact I wasn't going home.

'Where in the unkeelness are we going?'
shouted Bunky, speed-walking behind
me as I skateboarded through the
gates, towards Mogden High Street.
Nancy was running behind him, her
hair swishing like a cat's tail.

'Feeko's, of course!' I panted. 'To get
some Tears of Granny Laughter before
Gordon buys them all!'

I carried on skateboarding for another three and three-thirds of a minute, until we got to Feeko's. The doors whooshed open and I zigzagged down the aisles, straight to the Soft Drinks section. I skidded to a stop next to a cardboard cut-out of Irene from the Tears of Granny Laughter advert and grinned my grin I grin when I'm about to buy a carton of the keelest drink ever. Then I spotted Gordon Smugly.

Feeko's Mike

'Afternoon, Barold,' drawled Gordon, reaching out to grab a Tears of Granny Laughter, and I gasped.
I was gasping because the shelf was COMPERLEETERLY EMPTY apart from that carton.

'Oh dear, what a shame. None for little Barold!' he smiled, grabbing the carton and holding it up like he was in an advert for Tears of Granny Laughter.

The carton was Beryl flavour, which everyone knows is the tastiest Tears of Granny Laughter flavour, seeing as Beryl is the least ugly out of the three grannies in the advert.

Beryl
(not exackerly beautiful)

'NOOOOO!' I wailed, just as a skinny man in a Feeko's uniform popped his head around the aisle.

'Hello, my name's Mike. Let me see if I can find you another carton of Tears of Granny Laughter today!' chuckled the man, whose name tag said Mike, plus he'd just said his name was Mike, so I spose his name was Mike.

Mike

trying to play it keel

Mike pulled a screen out of his back pocket and started tapping on it with his finger. 'Okey-dokey, sold out there . . .' he mumbled, checking all the Feeko's in Mogden to see if they had any cartons left. 'Nope . . . nope . . . nope . . .' he frowned, and then his frown turned upside down and he looked up, the way a Mike looks up when he's found a Feeko's with some Tears of Granny Laughters in it.

turn book
upside down

'Two cartons left in Feeko's Funsize!' he grinned, as Gordon glided off towards the till.

Dog wee sofa

'Where are we going now?' shouted Nancy, as I zigzagged back down the aisles and out the whooshing doors towards Feeko's Funsize, which is where the last two cartons in the whole of Mogden were.

Feeko's Funsize is the keel mini Feeko's on Mogden Common, the bit of grass where everyone goes to let their dogs do poos.

'We've got to get to Mogden Common before Gordon!' I cried, turning right and zooming down an alleyway. 'Follow me, I know a short cut!'

At the end was a brick wall with an old sofa slumped in front of it, soaking wet from rain and dog wee. 'It's a dead end!' shouted Nancy, running up next to me with Bunky, and I turned my head and smiled, feeling like **Future Ratboy**.

'Watch this!' I grinned, aiming my skateboard at a plank of wood that was leaning against the sofa like a ramp. 'YIPPEE-KEEL-KAYAY!' I screamed, as I fast-forwarded up it and shot into the air.

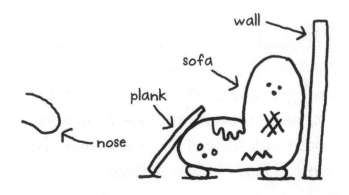

58

'CRUNK!' bent my nose, donking straight into the brick wall, and I flomped on to the sofa. 'Dime dokay ...' I said, clambering up the soggy cushions and over the wall, then crashing into a bush growing next to a dog poo bin.

'WEEEHEEE!' cried Bunky, plomping down next to the bush on a nice soft bit of grass with flowers growing out of it, and I wondered why it always worked out so well for everyone else but me. Then I heard a thud.

Talking to myself out loud

'AAARRRGGGHHH!!!' screamed Nancy, who was lying by the wall, holding her leg. 'MY ANKLE! I THINK IT'S BROKEN!'

Bunky leaped up and ran over to her as I scrambled out of the bush and jumped on my skateboard, pushing off towards Feeko's Funsize.

'What are you lot doing here?' said a familikeels voice out of nowhere, and I spotted Anton Mildew speed-walking past us towards the mini supermarket.

hair looks ← like tree

gasping

'Why is Anton speed-walking towards Feeko's Funsize?' I mumbled to myself, scratching my head.

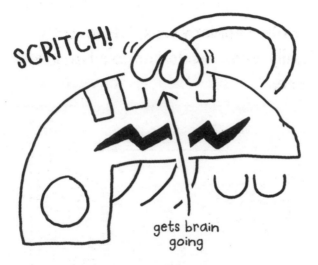

SCRITCH!

gets brain going

'A-HA!' I boomed, working it out. 'He must be after the last Tears of Granny Laughters too! Now I've got Gordon AND Anton to deal with!' I said. I don't know why I was talking out loud to myself so much, by the way.

'Not so fast, Mildew!' I blurted, zooming past him through the whooshing doors and into Feeko's Funsize.

The only problem was, I'd never actually been inside Feeko's Funsize before.

Beryl
and
Irene

I zogzigged down the aisles, darting my eyes around for Tears of Granny Laughter. 'Nope . . . nope . . . nope . . .' I muttered, reminding myself of Feeko's Mike, until I spotted a familiar-looking granny.

Facing me at the end of the aisle stood
a cardboard cut-out of Gertrude,
the ugliest of all the Tears of Granny
Laughter grannies.

Gertrude
cut-out

'Oh my keelness, are you a sight for
sore eyes!' I said, darting towards
Gertrude, the last two cartons of
Tears of Granny Laughter sitting on
the shelf next to her.

One of the cartons was Beryl flavour, which everyone knows is the tastiest, and the other was Irene, which everyone knows isn't. I reached my hand up for the Beryl and it bumped against another, non-Barryish hand.

'Not so fast, Loser!' warbled Anton Mildew.

Hand
scrabbles

'That's not fair, I got here first!' I shouted, scrabbling Anton's hand away from the carton of Beryl flavour Tears of Granny Laughter. Anton's hand scrabbled back, knocking the Irene flavour carton off the shelf, and I caught it.

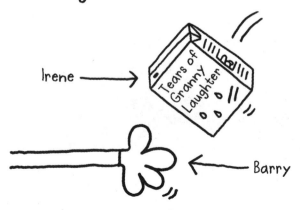

Irene →

Tears of Granny Laughter

← Barry

'Fine with me!' smiled Anton, lifting up the Beryl carton.

Just then Nancy limped round the corner, using Bunky as a walking stick. 'Thanks for all your help, Barry,' she groaned, giving me an evil stare, and I did my face I do when I haven't got time to say sorry.

'Anton stole my carton of Beryl!' I whined, in a whiney kind of way.

'What, this one?' said Bunky, snatching it out of his hand.

'Hey, that's not fair!' screamed Anton, and Bunky snatched the Irene one out of my hand too, just to make it fair.

Bunky looked at me and smiled his stupid smile. 'Now what, Barry?' he said, and right there on the spot I came up with one of my brilliant and amazing ideas.

The magic coin

I reached my hand into my pocket and pulled out the magic 50p. 'Let's flip my coin for the Beryl carton!' I said, tossing it in the air. 'Heads or tails, Anton?'

'Er, umm, ooh, I can't decide . . .'
warbled Anton, as the coin shimmered
in mid-air. 'Tails!' he shouted, as it
landed in my palm.

I peered into my hand and felt my
nose droop. 'Tails it is!' smiled Nancy.

smiling
through
the pain

reflection
in glasses

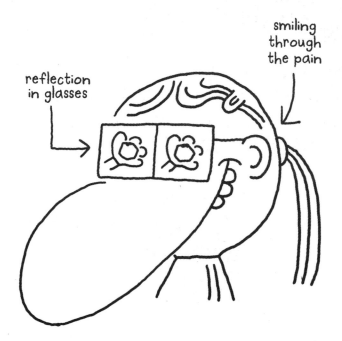

Bunky passed Anton his carton of Beryl. 'Oh well, at least I've GOT a Tears of Granny Laughter!' I said, opening my hand to grab my carton of Irene, and my magic 50p slipped out of my palm, bounced along the floor and rolled underneath the shelf.

'WAAAAH! MY COIN!' I screamed, dropping to my knees and scrabbling about underneath the shelves. 'Bunky, Nancy, help me look!' I cried, as Gordon Smugly's shoes appeared in front of my eyes.

Ten seconds

'We meet again, Barold,' burped Gordon's smug, ugly voice as I carried on scrabbling around for my coin. His burp drifted down towards my nostrils, smelling of the Beryl carton he'd bought earlier.

Beryl flavour

me scrabbling about

'Ooh, look what we have here, the very last carton of Tears of Granny Laughter!' he said, staring at the one in Bunky's hand and pulling a non-magic 50p out of his pocket.

MY carton of Irene

I stopped scrabbling for two milliseconds and peered up at Gordon's face.
'Please don't take my Tears of Granny Laughter, Gordon,' I begged. 'It's all I've got to live for!'

Gordon smiled his smile he smiles when he's enjoying watching someone scrabble around on the floor. 'I'll give you ten seconds. After that, the carton's mine,' he chuckled. 'Better get scrabbling, Loser!' he said, and he started counting down from ten.

'TEN!' I heard, as I slotted my hand back underneath the shelf and started scrabbling it around. 'NINE!' he boomed, and I felt something small and round and metal.

'Got it!' I shouted, pulling out a 1p.

'I'll let you have a sip of my Beryl carton for 1p!' chuckled Anton, at the same time as Gordon was shouting 'EIGHT'.

'Where in the unkeelness is it?' I sighed to myself, and my sigh blew a ball of dust the size of a bogie along the floor. The dust bogie rolled along, stopping when it bumped into a familiar-looking shape. 'My 50p!' I gasped, stretching my fingers out as far as they could go. 'C-can't . . . quite . . . r-reach . . .' I stuttered, not quite reaching it.

dust
bogie

I breathed out, flumping against the floor like one of Desmond's empty nappy bags. 'FOUR!' shouted Gordon, and I thought of my mum and dad at home, peering into Baby Des's eyes.

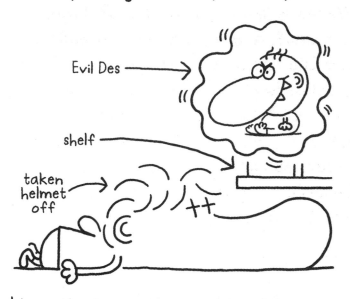

Evil Des

shelf

taken helmet off

I breathed in again, and tried to come up with another one of my brillikeel and amazepoos ideas. 'BY THE POWER OF KEELNESS!' I roared, and a plan popped into my head.

The magic straw

'Bunky, rip me off that straw!' I boomed, as Gordon opened his mouth to shout 'THREE'.

straw on back of Irene

'Eeve keelse!' smiled Bunky, ripping the straw off the carton of Irene and throwing it to me.

'Ungfh!' I blurted, diving to catch the straw and ripping it out of its plastic sleeve. I looked at the little pink tears dotted all over it and smiled, even though there really wasn't time for smiling at pink tears.

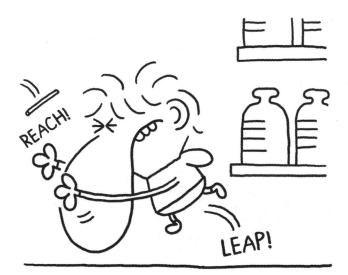
REACH!

LEAP!

I pincered the straw in my fingers and slid it underneath the shelf, trying to flick the 50p towards myself.

'. . . ONE!' boomed Gordon. 'Time's up, Barry!' he grinned, as I quadruple-reverse-waggle-flicked the straw and the 50p shot out from under the shelf.

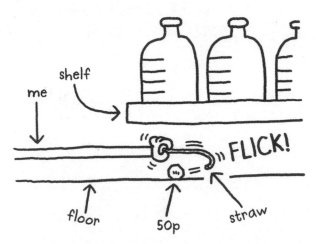

'Not so fast, Smugly!' I beamed, holding it up to his smug, ugly face, and Bunky passed me my carton.

Irene flavour Tears of Granny Laughter

'I'll get you for this, Barold!' wailed Gordon as I handed my magic 50p over to the cashier and carried the Irene flavour Tears of Granny Laughter out of Feeko's Funsize. Who cared if it wasn't a Beryl? I still had a carton of the keelest drink in Mogden.

'See you tomozkeels!' I shouted at the top of my road, as Nancy limped off, using Bunky as a zimmer frame, and I trundled up to my house.

I opened the door and immedikeely wished I didn't have any ears or noses.

chopped-off nose

nostril holes

just a hole

Desmond Loser the Second had stunk the house out with one of his poos and his screams were jiggling the china pigs on the mantelpiece.

My mum was in the bathroom with Desmond, changing his nappy. 'Barry, do me a favour and pass me that toilet roll, would you,' she said, not even asking what I'd done at school that day.

I've always hated it when my mum asks me what I've done at school that day, but now that she'd stopped, I sort of missed it.

'Guess what, Mum!' I smiled, holding up my carton. 'I got the last carton of Irene flavour Tears of Granny Laughter!' I was so excited, I'd forgotten she didn't want me drinking it.

'That's lovely, dear,' she said, not even listening. 'Now pass me that toilet roll, would you?'

I spun a metre of toilet paper off the roll and scrunched it into a ball, throwing it at my mum just as the phone started ringing.

DRRRRR!!!

'Get that, would you, Barry?' she said, and I swivelled round on the spot and flicked the phone out of its holder, rolling my eyes to myself.

'Loser residence,' I said into the little holes at the bottom of the phone.

'Ooh is that my little Barry Warry?' warbled Granny Harumpadunk's voice out the little holes at the top of the phone.

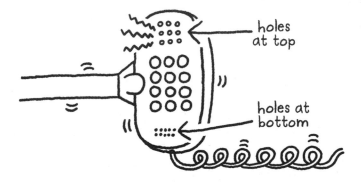

holes at top

holes at bottom

I put my hand over the little holes at the bottom of the phone so Granny Harumpadunk couldn't hear, and turned to my mum. 'It's Granny Harumpadunk,' I said, wondering why I didn't want Granny Harumpadunk hearing me say her name.

'Take Des would you, Barry,' said my mum, passing me Desmond and grabbing the phone. 'Hello, Sheila,' she said, because Granny Harumpadunk isn't her mum, she's my dad's.

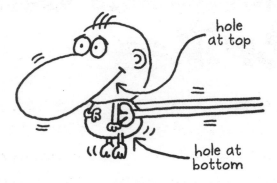

hole at top

hole at bottom

I waddled into the living room, carrying Desmond Loser the Second, who was peering into my eyes the way I peer into my cuddly **Future Ratboy's**. 'What?' I said, and he smiled, then giggled, then burped, then did a blowoff, then stuck his bottom lip out and started crying.

Disasteroid strikes

'Nope, nope, nope . . .' I noped, sounding like Feeko's Mike again. The last thing I needed was Desmond wailing down my earholes when all I wanted to do was put my feet up and drink my carton of Irene flavour Tears of Granny Laughter in peace and quiet.

I plonked my bum on the bouncy ball my mum uses when she does her yoga and started boinging Desmond up and down. ' "He's the keelest at playing it keeeeeel" . . .' I sang, singing the theme tune to **Future Ratboy**.

'WAAAAHHHH!!!' screamed Desmond, his whole face turning into a mouth.

'Look Des, it's a carton of Irene flavour Tears of Granny Laughter!' I cooed, picking up my favourite thing in the whole wide universe amen.

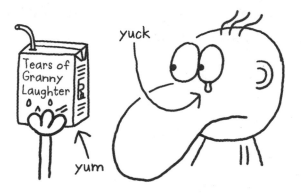

yuck

Tears of Granny Laughter

yum

Desmond Loser the Second stopped crying and looked at the little straw with pink tears dotted all over it, which I'd already poked through the foil circle on the top of the carton. 'BLURGLE!' he smiled, reaching out to grab it, and I pulled my hand away, knocking something off the mantelpiece behind me.

I swivelled round on the bouncy ball and spotted one of my mum's little pigs flying towards the fireplace tiles. 'NOOOOO!!!' I screamed, reaching out to catch it. The even-laster thing I needed was my mum shouting at me about a smashed-up pig.

The only problem with reaching out to catch a flying pig when you've got a Baby Des in one hand and a carton of Irene in the other is you've only got two hands.

'Sorry Irene!' I cried, dropping the carton, because I couldn't really drop my own baby brother, and I bounced off the yoga ball towards the pig.

SMASH! It slipped through my fingers and broke into ten pieces.

'Oh. My. Unkeelness,' I whisper-shouted. But the worst bit was still about to happen.

Squidged Irene

'Bye, Sheila!' I heard my mum warble as she hung up and started walking towards the living room.

I plonked Baby Des on the sofa and dived towards Irene, who was lying on the tiles. I'd remembered my mum didn't like me drinking it, and I didn't want her to take it off me.

'BY THE POWER OF KEELNESS!' I roared,
crashing nose first into the fireplace,
which luckeely for me is one of those
fake fireplaces that only has vases of
dried flowers in them.

Super
Barry

dried
flowers

Irene

Unluckeely for me, my foot landed RIGHT ON TOP OF Irene. SPLURGE! exploded the carton, squirting Irene tears all over the dried flowers.

dried flowers over here

FFFT!

STOMP!

'NOOOOOOO!!!' I screamed. The dried flowers weren't dry any more. And my carton of Tears of Granny Laughter was comperleeterly empty.

Blaming Desmond

'What in the name of Great Uncle Desmond is going on here?' screeched my mum, her shadow making everything go dark.

I picked up my squidged carton of Irene and held it in my arms. 'Oh my poor, sweet Irene,' I sobbed, as my mum barged past me and scooped up Des, who'd stopped wailing and was sleeping like a baby.

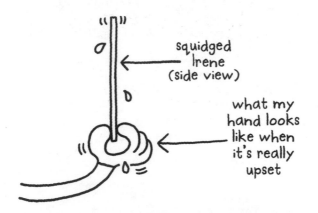

squidged Irene (side view)

what my hand looks like when it's really upset

My mum spotted my carton and gasped. 'Barry, what did I tell you about drinking that awful stuff!' she shouted. She bent over and picked up the little pig's curly tail, holding it between her fingers like a worm poo.

'My piggy!' she screeched, and she spotted her soaking wet dried flowers. 'My flowers!' she shrieked, and Desmond started to cry.

wet dried flowers *

*sorry about how boring this pic is

I dropped to my knees and started crying too, seeing as the one thing I had to live for had just been squashed flat by my own foot. 'It's all Des's fault!' I wailed, stroking my flattened-out carton.

'Don't you start blaming your little brother, young man,' barked my mum, kissing Desmond's head, and we stared at each other, both of us stroking our babies.

'I wish Desmond Loser the Second was never born!' I boomed, crawling between my mum's legs towards the stairs, and I stomped up to my room and curled up in bed.

Morning poo poo

My dad was shaving in the upstairs bathroom the next morning and my mum was changing Desmond's nappy in the downstairs one as per usual, so I left for school without doing my morning poo.

storming
off
again

'We need to talk, Barry!' called my mum as I slammed the front door shut, comperleeterly ignoring her.

'Where's Nancy?' I said, blowing off as I bumped into Bunky at the top of my road.

'She can't walk!' smiled Bunky, like it was the best thing ever. 'The doctors put her foot in a cast and said she couldn't go to school for a whole week. How was your carton of Irene?' he said, all in one go.

I thought of Irene, lying squidged on my pillow at home, and put my hand into my pocket. I'd picked the straw up out of the fireplace that morning and plopped it in my trousers, to keep me company.

'I don't want to talk about it,'
I mumbled, giving the straw a little strokeypoos, and we walked to school in silence, apart from the noise of my blowoffs.

Mrs Wisses

'Lovely day, isn't it!' smiled the art teacher, Mrs Wisses, when we got to school, and everyone nodded apart from me.

Mrs Wisses isn't our normal teacher,
Miss Spivak is. But Miss Spivak was
away for a week, so we had
Mrs Wisses as our teacher instead.

where
Miss Spivak
was

'Today you can draw whatever you
like!' she said, slotting a prawn cocktail
flavour crisp into her mouth.

I looked around for the quickest thing to draw, seeing as I wasn't really in a drawing sort of mood, and decided on the blowoff floating up from under my desk. 'Fi-nished,' I said, signing it at the bottom, and Anton Mildew opened his mouth.

FFFT!

my autograph, remember?

Barry

'I know what I can draw!' he said, scrabbling about in his rucksack and lifting out a blue metal box with a yellow lock on the front. He stuck his hand in his pocket and pulled out a tiny key, poked it into the lock and twisted.

'Behold, the last of the Beryls!' he beamed, slipping a pair of white cotton gloves on to his hands and lifting the lid. Inside, surrounded by cotton wool, sat his carton of Beryl. 'Please don't stare directly at the carton,' he warbled, as everyone gathered round.

DO. NOT.
LOOK. AT.

Darren Darrenofski slurped on the Tropical Mango and Coconut Fronkle he was drawing. 'I wouldn't look at it even if you paid me a million Fronkles,' he burped, looking straight at the carton, and Sharonella bonked him on the nose.

'Where's your carton of Irene, Barry?' smiled Anton.

'I don't want to talk about it,' I sighed, holding in my poo at the same time.

The Poo Hold-In
(© Barry Loser)

Bunky stopped drawing his drawing of Darren's drawing and turned around. 'That's what he said to me too!' he said, and I rolled my eyes to myself.

'All that scrabbling around on your hands and knees to find your filthy little 50p, and now you don't even want to talk about your precious carton?' sneered Gordon Smugly, not even looking at me. He was too busy peering into a mirror, sketching his smug, ugly face.

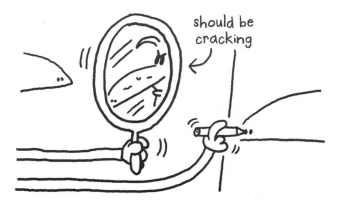

should be cracking

'Yeah Barry, talk to Shazza, it'll make you feel better!' smiled Sharonella, and she swaggered over, wafting her stinking perfume up my nostrils.

'I DROPPED IT AND TROD ON IT AND THE WHOLE THING SQUIRTED ALL OVER MY MUM'S STUPID DRIED FLOWERS, OK?!' I screamed, and I was just getting ready to hear everyone laugh when the fire alarm started clanging.

CLAAANG!!!

FIRE Ø ALARM

Clenching my bum

'Do not panic, children,' choked Mrs Wisses, getting up from her chair and stuffing the rest of her prawn cocktail crisps in her mouth. 'I'm sure this is just a practice alarm!'

She slurped her tea and pointed at the door out to the playground, which was already open with everyone screaming and running through.

Anton picked his carton of Beryl up and started putting it away in its box. 'Not so fast, Mildew,' spluttered Mrs Wisses. 'Everything stays exactly where it is during the fire alarm, thank you very much,' she shouted, stuffing a packet of cheese and onion crisps into her pocket and grabbing her coat and bag.

'B-but Mrs Wisses, you don't understand,' stuttered Anton. 'I can't leave Beryl here . . .'

splutter   stutter

Mrs Wisses slung her bag over her shoulder and marched Anton out of the classroom. 'I'm sure Beryl will be fine,' she chuckled, shaking her head as if he'd gone stark raving bonkoids.

I waddled out behind them, clenching my bum together so I didn't do a poo right there and then on the spot, and got in line behind Bunky.

'Nothing to worry about, children, this is just a false alarm,' boomed Mr Koops, the sports teacher, and everyone groaned.

'All that for nothing,' whined Anton, whose voice is pretty whiney anyway. 'If anything happens to Beryl . . .'

Gordon chuckled and opened his smugly mouth. 'I wouldn't worry, Mildew,' he drawled, looking over at me. 'At least it's still full . . . unlike Barold's!' he laughed, and I felt a blowoff trying to squeeze its way out of my bum.

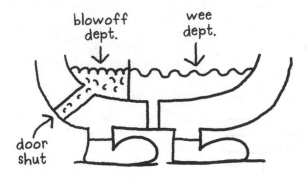

blowoff dept.

wee dept.

door shut

'Shut your mouth, Smugly!' I shouted, and the blowoff popped out.

Darren Darrenofski was standing behind me, so he was the first to smell it. 'POOWEE!' he screamed, spitting Tropical Mango and Coconut Fronkle into Sharonella's face.

x-ray of blowoff going into Darren

'PPFFAHH!!' cried Sharonella, spinning round and bonking noses with Bunky.

'What's going on here?' spluttered Mrs Wisses, spraying cheese and onion flavour crisp crumbs into Anton's hair, and I zagzogged off towards the toilets, before it was comperleeterly too late.

The toilet roll mirakeel

'Aaahhh, thank keelness for that!' I smiled, as I reached out for the toilet roll. I was in the furthest cubicle along in the boys' toilets, which is my favourite spot for emergency poos like the one I'd just done.

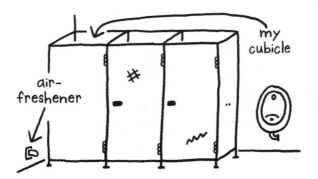

air-freshener

my cubicle

The smell of a plug-in air-freshener wafted under the cubicle door and mixed in with my poo, making quite a nice smell actually, thank you very much indeed amen.

Suddenly my smile turned upside down. 'Nope . . . Nope . . . NOPE!!!' I cried, sounding like Feeko's Mike, except more panicky. 'THERE'S NO TOILET ROLLLLL!!' I shrieked, which is the worst sentence you can say out loud in the history of saying sentences out loud.

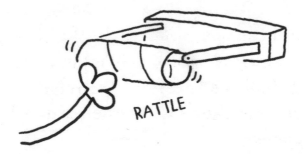

RATTLE

I closed my eyes and scrunched my brain up, trying to squeeze one of my brilliant and amazoid ideas out. 'By the power of keelness!' I cried, but it was no use, I couldn't think of anything.

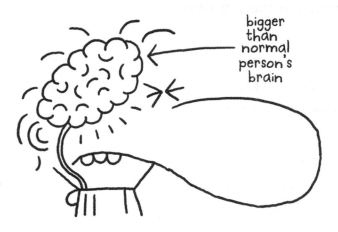

bigger than normal person's brain

I put my head in my hands and stared at the little gap that goes all the way round the bottom edge of the cubicle, wondering if I could slide underneath and steal the toilet roll from next door. And that's when the mirakeel happened.

At first all I saw was a flash of white appearing under the door. 'It's nothing Barry, you're just going bonkoids,' I whispered to myself.

Then I saw the whole end of a toilet roll poking into the cubicle, like a pig's snout except with only one nostril.

if pigs had toilet roll snouts

I reached out to grab it, but it disappeared again, and I heard a little sniggle. 'OK, very funny. Now pass me the toilet roll!' I said, wondering if I really had gone comperleeterly bonkoids.

The toilet roll poked its snout under the door again and this time it stayed there.

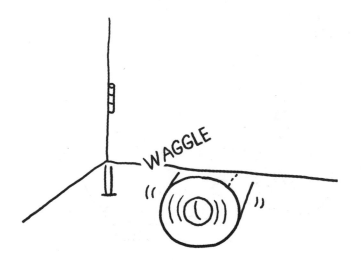

'Thank you, whoever you are!' I beamed, and I grabbed the toilet roll and wiped my bum and flushed the toilet.

I creaked the cubicle door open and peered out into the room. 'Hel-loo, any-bo-dy ther-ere?' I cooed, but everything was normal. Apart from the plug-in air-freshener had disappeared!

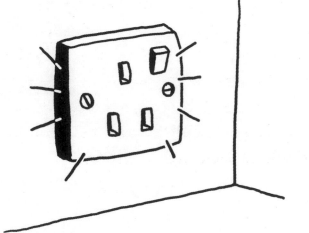

The crumpled carton

I was the first one back in the classroom, so I put my feet up on the desk and thought about how loserish my life had been recently. First my stupid baby brother had stolen my mum and dad, and now I was never going to taste my favourite drink in the whole wide world amen.

'Oh well, I spose it can't get any worse,'
I muttered to myself, feeling sleepy, so
I closed my eyes.

The next thing I knew, Anton was
screaming in my face. 'MY TEARS OF
GRANNY LAUGHTER!' he cried. 'YOU
DRANK MY PRECIOUS BERYL!'

I opened my eyes and realised I must have nodded off. 'How in the why what when who where which?' I said, not knowing what the unkeelness was going on.

Anton was holding his carton of Beryl, his hands shaking. The little hole at the top had been pierced, and one side was comperleeterly crumpled up, just like my Irene. I could smell Beryl's tears wafting out of the little hole, and my nostrils did a snuffle, like a dog's.

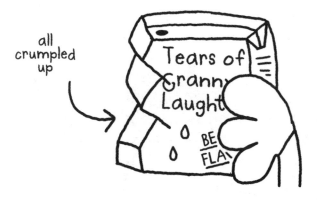

all crumpled up

Tears of Granny Laught

BE FLA

'It wasn't me!' I said, wondering if I'd sleep-drunk it without realising, and I swiped my tongue around my mouth to see if it tasted of anything, which it didn't, apart from boring old spit.

what spit tastes like ———→ (nothing)

The whole class had gathered behind Anton, staring at me like I was a baddy in an episode of Detective Manksniff. 'Barold, Barold, Barold,' Gordon smiled. 'I know you were upset about your own carton being squidged, but you didn't have to drink Anton's!' he sneered.

My ears couldn't believe themselves. 'Th-that's not true!' I wailed, in a waily kind of way. 'S-somebody must've drunk it before I came back in!' I said, wondering how I hadn't noticed the crumpled carton earlier, seeing as I'm the world's number one expert at spotting cartons of Tears of Granny Laughter.

award for being best at spotting things

Anton collapsed to the floor sobbing, Tears of Anton Sadness pouring out of his eyes, and Mrs Wisses wobbled over.

'Children, children, children,' she spluttered, tearing open a packet of salt and vinegar crisps. 'What IS going on?'

CRINKLE

RUSTLE

'Barry killed Beryl!' burped Darren, pointing at the crumpled carton and then at me, and Mrs Wisses shook her head like she thought the whole class had gone stark raving bonkeroids.

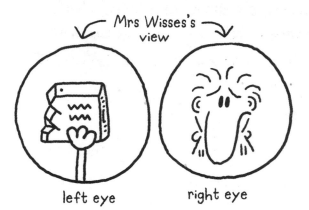

left eye   right eye

'Is this true, Loser?' she said, bending down and peering into my eyes the way Detective Manksniff peers into a baddy's.

'No,' I mumbled, not that it was going to make any difference.

Desmond Loser the Worst

A brand new stack of Daily Poos towered next to the school gates as I trundled through them with Bunky five hours, twenty-seven minutes and thirty-four seconds later, heading for home.

Bunky picked up a copy and looked at the front cover. 'BARRY LOSER DRINKS ANTON'S LAST BERYL!' boomed the headline, with a photo of the crumpled carton underneath.

He folded the paper in half and stuffed it in his back pocket, not saying anything at all. He'd been acting weird like that all day, looking at me out of the corner of his eye like he thought I'd drunk Anton's carton of Beryl when I comperleeterly hadn't.

'Poor little old keelness me,' I sighed, carrying a pile of homework to deliver to Nancy, which was my punishment from Mrs Wisses. 'My mum and dad don't love me, the whole class thinks I'm a liar, and I STILL haven't tasted Tears of Granny Laughter . . .'

bad mood

'I don't think you're a liar, Barry,' said Bunky, but I comperleeterly didn't believe him.

'Tell Nancy I'll be round later,' I said at the top of my road, and Bunky gave me a mini-salute from inside his pocket.

not that I could see it

'At least my mum doesn't know about Anton's carton,' I mumbled to myself as I opened the front door and saw my mum standing in the hallway carrying Desmond in one hand and the phone in the other. 'Thank you for telling me about Anton's carton, Mrs Wisses,' she said, hanging up and giving me an evil stare.

'I-it's not true! I didn't drink Beryl!' I cried, but I could tell she didn't believe me.

'If it's not one thing it's the other with you, isn't it, Barry?' she said, stroking Des's cheek.

one thing

the other

'Oh I'm so sorry I'm not perfect like Desmond Loser the WORST!' I screamed, secretly quite pleased with my nickname for Des, even though WORST rhymes with FIRST, not SECOND, so it's not exackerly perfect.

Desmond stuck his bottom lip out and started to grumble. 'I haven't got time for this, Barry,' sighed my mum. 'Your gran's down at Mogden Hall setting up the jumble sale for Saturday. Why don't you go and help her,' she said.

So I grabbed Nancy's homework and headed for Mogden Hall, which was on the way to her house.

Very loud nattering indeed

I opened the door to Mogden Hall and felt like I'd walked into Desmond's mouth in the middle of one of his screams. Eight million grannies, all of them identikeel, were unpacking boxes and nattering to each other at the same time.

Mr Hodgepodge was up on stage, practising his magic show. His shaky hand was holding a saw over a coffin-sized box, and he was talking to Granny Harumpadunk. She was dressed in her glamorous assistant's costume, which was a spangly gold leotard with a yellow tutu, and feathers in her hair.

'. . . then you climb into the box and I chop you in half!' smiled The Great Hodgepodge, looking at the coffin.

Madame Harumpadunk smoothed
her feathers down and mumbled to
herself nervously.

'Granny!' I shouted, and she smiled.

'Coowee, Barry Warry!' she cried,
tottering down the steps from the
stage, looking relieved to get away
from Mr Hodgepodge.

'My mum sent me down to help,'
I grumbled, flipping my skateboard up
and slotting it under my arm with the
pile of Nancy's homework.

Granny Harumpadunk's best friend
Ethel trundled over in her wheelchair
and ruffled my hair, peering into my
eyes through her greasy glasses. 'Ooh,
is that our little Barry? Last time I saw
you, you were this high!' she croaked,
holding her hand up about three
millimetres lower than the top of my
head, because I'd only seen her last
week.

'What's wrong, Barry?' said Granny Harumpadunk, cuddling me into her spangly leotard, and the spangles scraped against my cheek. Granny Harumpadunk's good like that, always knowing when I'm upset about something, which is most of the time.

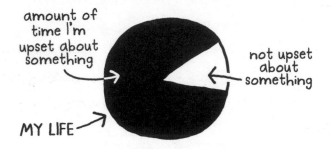

amount of time I'm upset about something

not upset about something

MY LIFE →

'Oh, you wouldn't understand,' I mumbled. 'It's just that my carton of Irene got squidged, and I was doing a poo when the toilet roll ran out, then I fell asleep in the classroom and when I woke up, Anton said I'd drunk his Beryl,' I jabbered, all in one breath.

I looked around at the grannies, waiting for them to start shaking their heads to themselves like I'd gone stark raving bonkoids.

'Ooh, that blooming Anton!' warbled Granny Harumpadunk, cuddling me tighter.

'Outrageous! As if our Barry would do a thing like that!' scoffed Ethel, pulling a Detective-Manksniff-style hat out of a box.

some old grandad's

GRAB!

'You've got to get out there and prove they're wrong, Barry, that's what you've got to do!' shouted The Great Hodgepodge from the stage, and he waggled his eyebrows at my Granny. 'Excuse me, Madame Harumpadunk, but I can't practise chopping you in half when you're standing around nattering,' he said, and Granny Harumpadunk sighed.

WAGGLE

SHAKE

'Hodge is right, Barry, you've got to fight for your name,' she mumbled, clip-clopping up the steps in her high heels, and before I knew it Ethel had marched me out of the front door and plonked the Detective Manksniff hat on my head for good luck.

PLONK!

on top of helmet

Round Nancy's

I stood outside Mogden Hall and looked up at the sky. 'Now what?' I muttered to myself, wondering how somebody goes about fighting for their name, especially when their name's as loserish as mine is. Then I remembered Nancy's homework.

'Nancy'll know what to do!' I said, zooming round her house in three seconds flat and knocking on her door, doing my face I do when a door's about to open.

door face

(taken helmet off)

'Hello, Barry,' sighed Mrs Verkenwerken, sounding tired, and a familiar-looking toddler appeared behind her in a stroller.

I peered down at the toddler and flicked through my brain, trying to remember his name. The last time I'd seen Nancy's brother he was still a tiny little baby, just like Desmond.

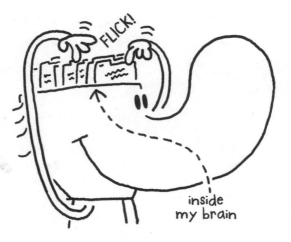

FLICK!

inside
my brain

'Keith Verkenwerken!' I smiled, pushing my hat back, and I glanced at Nancy's mum, to make sure I'd got it right. 'Why, aren't you a swell little fella!' I said in my Detective Manksniff voice, and a brilliant and amazekeel idea popped out of my head into my hat.

'That's it!' I mumbled to myself, scrabbling my hand about in my pocket. I pulled out the Irene straw I'd been carrying around for company and stuck it between my lips, just like Detective Manksniff does when he's trying to solve one of his mysteries. 'I'll become a detective and find out who crumpled Anton's carton!'

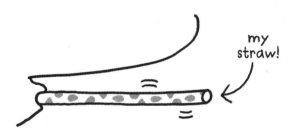

my straw!

Keith rolled off down the hall, comperleeterly not interested in my idea at all. 'Nancy's in her room,' said Mrs Verkenwerken, running after him, and I bounded up the stairs on all fours.

Nancy was sitting in front of her bedroom window, her bad leg propped up on a stool. The sun was setting behind her, so all I could see was her silhouette. She was stroking her pet cat, Gregor, and reading a big green book with X-rays of human bones in it.

my view

'Barry, so nice of you to visit,' she murmured, stroking the cat like a film baddy, and I started to worry she hated me for not helping when she hurt her foot.

'How you feeling, Nance?' I said, and Gregor hissed.

HISSSSSSSSSS!!!

Nancy's eyebrows flickered and my heart started to jump. 'Fine!' she smiled, looking up from her book, and I sighed with relief. The door behind me opened and I quickly did my door face, turning round to see Bunky walking through it, zipping up his flies.

'Oh. Hi Barry,' he said, giving me a look like he thought I'd drunk Anton's carton.

I turned back to Nancy, who was reading her X-ray book like nothing had happened. 'Spose Bunky's told you all about today,' I said, trying to see if she thought I was guilty too.

'No, he hasn't said anything about it . . .' she said, which I thought was weird, seeing as it was the biggest news ever.

'Well . . .' I said, and I started to tell her everything that had happened, which was really boring for me and Bunky, seeing as we'd already heard it all before.

Barry Loser, Private Detective

'. . . and that's why I've become Detective Loser,' I smiled, once I'd finished explaining everything to Nancy.

'Verrrrry interesting . . .' said Nancy, closing her book. Bunky was standing on the other side of the room, feeding Nancy's fish and not really taking any notice.

looks like Mogden Hall

'I didn't do it, honest to keelness I didn't, Nancy!' I warbled, picking up a pen and signing the cast on her foot.

'I believe you, Barry,' she said, peering out the window. 'The question is, who DID drink the carton . . . and WHY?'

I finished writing my name and drew a cartoon of myself in my detective hat, making my nose a bit shorter than it is in real life. Gregor jumped off Nancy's lap and strolled over to Bunky, meowing and stretching out his paw.

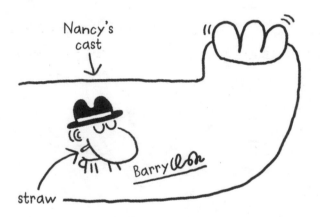

Nancy's cast

straw

Barry

'Maybe it was someone who wanted revenge?' Nancy muttered to herself. 'Sharonella, for example . . .'

I turned to Nancy and smiled. 'Go on . . .'
I said, chewing on my straw.

'Well, Anton said she was the Phantom
Air-Freshener Thief, remember. Maybe
she drank his Tears of Granny
Laughter to get him back for that?'
Nancy picked up my pen and poked it
down the side of her cast to scratch
her ankle.

'Yes . . . yes, of course!' I cried, looking
over at Bunky. He was flicking his foot
at Gregor, trying to stop the cat
pawing at his legs.

MEOW!

'I'm not saying it's definitely her,' said Nancy, pushing her glasses on to her forehead and rubbing her eyes. 'There's loads of people in our class. I'll have to give this some more thought tonight.'

She put her book down and wheeled her chair over to her desk with her good foot, not that her chair was a wheelchair, it was just a chair that had little wheels on it.

'That's right, Nancy. You have a good long think about it,' I said, grabbing Bunky's arm. 'Meanwhile, me and Bunky'll go ask Shazza a few questions!'

Round Sharonella's

It was getting dark as we turned up at Sharonella's house and I knocked on her door, doing my door face while I waited for it to open.

'What's all this about?' said Sharonella, opening the door, and I took my hat off and walked in, almost fainting from the smell of her perfume.

cloud of perfume

'Oh, nothing out of the ordinary . . . just thought we'd pop in and say hello,' I smiled, chewing on my straw, and we followed her into the kitchen. 'Evening, ma'am,' I said to Sharonella's gran in my Detective Manksniff voice. 'Mind if I talk to Sharonella for a second?'

'Do what you like, love!' croaked Sharonella's gran, who also stank of perfume. 'We're just sorting some stuff out for the jumble sale, aren't we, Shaz. You boys like a drink?' she grinned.

Me and Bunky nodded, and she lifted two tiny glasses out of a jumble sale box. 'Hope these'll do,' she said, pouring a centimetre of Cream Soda Fronkle into each one.

CLINK!

I picked mine up and led Sharonella into the lounge, leaving Bunky to chat to Sharonella's gran. 'You know why I'm here,' I whisper-shouted, drinking my cream soda and slamming the glass down on the coffee table, and a budgie squawked from inside a cage in the corner of the room.

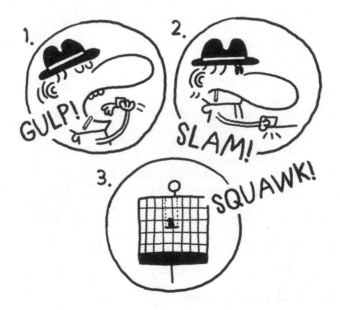

'Ooh Barry, I thought this day would never come!' warbled Sharonella, fluttering her eyelashes. 'Yes, of course I'll marry you!' she giggled, falling into my arms, and we crashed on to the sofa.

more of a dive really

'Cut the funny business, Shazza!' I shouted, wriggling out from under her and standing back up. 'I'm talking about Anton's carton of Beryl. I know you're the one who drank it!'

Sharonella's giggle turned into more of an annoyed chuckle. 'Oh don't be so ridiculous, Bazza!' she scoffed. 'As if I'd drink Anton's stupid drink!'

She turned away from me and looked through the window at the moon, which was hanging in the sky like a sideways smile. 'Besides, I wasn't in the classroom, and I can prove it!' she said.

'Perlease, be my guest!' I sighed, flumping down on the sofa again and pushing my hat back on my head. I was beginning to quite like wearing my detective hat, what with all the pushing it back on your head you can do.

FLUMP!

Sharonella took a breath and scrunched her face up so it looked a bit more loserish. '"Ooh, help me, I've done a poo and there's no toilet roll!"' she warbled, waggling her arms around like me when I've run out of toilet roll.

I thought back to earlier that day, when I'd been in the toilet doing my poo. 'H-how do you know about that?' I said, almost chewing through my straw.

'Because it was me who passed you the toilet roll, you luvverly great big loser!' chuckled Sharonella.

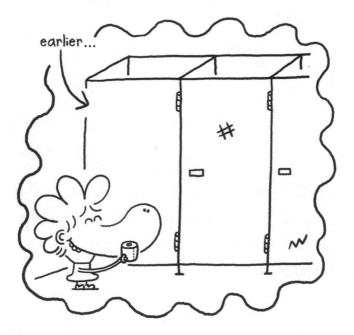

earlier...

I pulled my hat down over my eyes and thought for a millisecond. On the one hand, this was the most embarrassing thing that had ever happened to me in my whole entire life amen. But on the other . . .

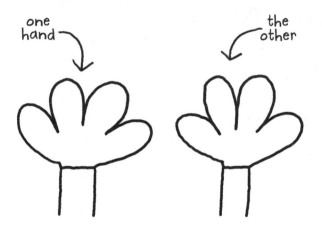

one
hand

the
other

'This is the keelest news ever!' I smiled, and I got ready to tell Sharonella exackerly why.

Unkeelest news ever

'Don't you see what this means?!'
I cried, standing up and grabbing
Sharonella by both shoulders. 'It means
you can tell people exackerly where I
was when Anton's carton was being
drunk!'

Sharonella looked at me like I was an idiot, which is how she usually looks at me anyway. 'Sorry Bazza, not gonna happen,' she said, crossing her arms and scowling at the budgie.

'Why the keelness not?' I wailed, and the budgie squawked, fluffing up his feathers.

'Think about it, Bazza. How's it gonna look when I say I was in the boys' toilets?' Sharonella squawked, but not fluffing up her feathers. 'I've got my keelness to think about, unlike you.'

'Hang on a milliminute . . . why WERE you in the boys' toilets?' I said, wondering why I hadn't wondered that to begin with.

wondering
about
not
wondering

Sharonella's cheeks went pink and she turned away again. 'Oh, erm . . . well . . .' she stuttered, peering at the moon. 'Darren sprayed me in the face with Fronkle, remember, and the girls' toilets were locked, you see . . . I needed somewhere to clean up, so I thought I'd just pop into the boys' . . .'

even moon doesn't believe her

I smiled to myself, the way
Detective Manksniff smiles when he
can tell someone's lying. Then I gasped.

I was gasping because behind
Sharonella, plugged into the plug
socket in the wall, was a plug-in
air-freshener.

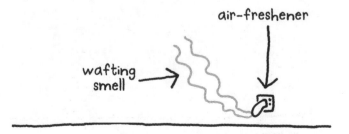

The Phantom Air-Freshener Thief

'Oh my unkeelness, you ARE the
Phantom Air-Freshener Thief, aren't
you!' I cried. I darted my eyes around
the room at all the plug sockets. Every
single one of them had a plug-in
air-freshener plugged into it.

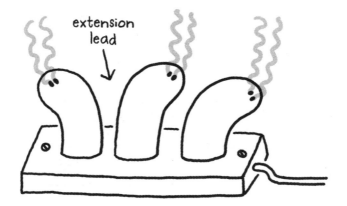

extension
lead

Sharonella twizzled round and hurried over to me, a droplet of sweat zogzagging down her forehead. 'Pleeeease Bazza, you can't tell anyone!' she begged, her perfume floating up my nostrils.

that zogzaggy sweat drop I just talked about

'Your perfume! That's air-freshener too, isn't it!' I laughed, my straw waggling in my mouth.

'It's my gran, she can't get enough of the stuff,' cried Sharonella. 'Plus if I didn't bring it home the whole place'd stink of budgie!' she squawked, pointing at the cage, and her budgie's beak drooped.

BEAK DROOP!

Bunky walked in with his empty glass, looking for somewhere to put it down. 'Even more disgustering than Tears of Granny Laughter!' he was saying to himself, looking at his half-drunk Cream Soda Fronkle.

'Please Barry, don't tell anyone . . . For me?' whispered Sharonella, and I did my Detective Manksniff smile.

'What's in it for me?' I said, twizzling my moustache, even though I don't have one.

me with moustache when I'm grown up

'Air-freshener?' said Sharonella, pulling one out of the wall and offering it to me.

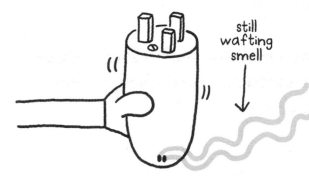

still wafting smell

I looked at her hand, and remembered it passing me the toilet roll. 'OK Shazza, I'll do it for you,' I sighed, waving the air-freshener away. 'Some detective I'm turning out to be . . .' I said, and that's when Sharonella's gran shuffled into the living room, looking at Bunky's bum. Which sounds a bit weird until you realise why.

The reason why

'Ooh, what's the latest gossip?' said Sharonella's gran, pointing at the Daily Poo sticking out of Bunky's back pocket, and Sharonella whipped it out of his trousers, holding the front cover up to her granny's glasses.

'BARRY LOSER DRINKS ANTON'S LAST BERYL,' warbled Sharonella's gran, reading the headline out loud. 'Ooh, you are a naughty boy, Bazza!' she said, zooming her eyes in on the photo of the carton. 'Hey, and you're a lefty too!' she smiled. 'High five!'

Sharonella's gran held her shaky left hand up in the air, and I did my face I do when I don't know what the unkeelness someone is talking about.

er, high four more like?

'What in the unkeelness are you talking about, Sharonella's gran?' I said, scratching my head with my right hand, seeing as I'm right-handed.

'You're left-handed!' grinned Sharonella's gran, pointing at the photo with her left hand. 'You can tell from the way you crumpled Anton's carton after you drank it!'

Photo by Gaspar Pink

'Er, hello? I'm no-ot?' I said, pointing at my right hand with my left one, but Sharonella's gran just ignored me. I Future-Ratboy-zoomed my eyes in on the carton and waggled my eyebrows. Sharonella's gran was right! The carton was only crumpled on the left-hand side.

I pushed my hat back on my head with my right hand and clicked two of my fingers together. 'That's it!' I said. 'Sharonella's gran, I think you've cracked the case of the crumpled carton!'

or is it?

Roll up, roll up

It was the next day and me and Bunky
were wheeling Nancy through the
school gates in Ethel's wheelchair, which
I'd borrowed off Ethel for the
morning so that Nancy could come to
school with us.

'Roll up, roll up!' I shouted, getting everyone to roll up, which was the first part of my amazeypoos idea. 'Come and sign Nancy's cast, one at a time!'

doesn't even want her cast signed

Anton Mildew wobbled over, his eyes all puffy from crying the whole night long. 'I can't believe you're still friends with HIM,' he said to Nancy, plopping the lid off a pen and writing 'BARRY LOSER DRANK MY BERYL' on her cast.

'Yes, it surprises me too, Verkenwerken,'
warbled Gordon Smugly, gliding over.
'I thought you had better taste in
men,' he said, snatching the pen off
Anton in his LEFT HAND and moving it
towards Nancy's leg.

'AHA, I KNEW IT!' I boomed, because I'd
caught the left-handed carton crumpler!

'Knew what?' smiled Gordon, switching the pen into his right hand and squiggling his smug, ugly signature.

(secretly
bit jealous
of it)

'Erm . . .' I muttered, trying to think of something to say. 'I knew that that Fronkle ringpull over there on the pavement would still be in the same spot today as it was yesterday,' I said, comperleeterly making it up on the spot.

'That's cos it's glued down,' burped Darren Darrenofski, wobbling over, slurping on a can of Kiwi Fronkle. 'I did it last week to fool people into thinking they could pick it up,' he said, and I did a mini-salute to myself in my pocket for making something up that turned out to be comperleeterly true.

that glued-down ringpull I was just talking about

don't know who this is

'Erm, I haven't got a pen,' burped Darren, crumpling his Fronkle can in his LEFT HAND and throwing it over his shoulder.

'Pick that up!' shouted Mrs Wisses, walking past, and it landed straight in a bin, so that shut her up.

I pulled a pen out of my pocket and passed it to Darren, trying not to get too excited. Maybe Darren's left-handed Fronkle-crumple had been an accident. After all, his right hand HAD been busy picking a bogie out of one of his nostrils.

Darren grabbed the pen off me with his bogie fingers and my nose drooped with disappointment. THEN HE PASSED IT TO HIS CRUMPLE HAND. 'D-darren, you're not a lefty, are you?' I stuttered.

'Eeve keelse!' he grinned, signing his name on Nancy's cast with his LEFT HAND!

DARREN DARRENOFSKI

The right to remain unkeel

'Darren Darrenofski, I arrest you for
drinking Anton's Beryl and crumpling
it up with your left hand!' I boomed,
grabbing his arm and marching him off
towards Anton. 'You have the right to
remain unkeel!' I smiled, looking around
at the crowd that had started to
gather.

Darren wriggled free and turned to face me. 'What in the name of Caffeine-Free Diet Cherry Fronkle?' he burped, and the smell of kiwi wafted up my nostrils.

BUUURRRPPP!!!

'Tell him, Nancy,' I said, and Nancy explained all about Sharonella's gran working out about the left-handed crumpler, which was pret-ty boring for me, Bunky and Sharonella, seeing as we'd heard it all before.

'Ooh, it was crumpled by a lefty!' scoffed Darren, cracking open a can of Bubblegum Fronkle with his left hand. 'Big deal! I wouldn't drink a carton of Tears of Granny Laughter if you paid me a million Fronkles!' he burped.

Darren's burp wafted into the air, and I imagined a bird flying through it and fainting from the stink.

'I think he's telling the truth, Barry,'
said Nancy, from Ethel's wheelchair.
I pulled my hat over my eyes and tried
to think.

PULL

'Face it, Barry,' drawled a smug, ugly
voice, and I looked up. 'You drank
Anton's carton and everyone knows
it!' smiled Gordon Smugly.

I looked around at the crowd and held
my arms out, begging them to believe
me. 'I didn't kill Beryl!' I wailed, feeling
my legs go wobbly.

Bunky stepped forwards and put his hand on my shoulder. 'I believe you, Barry,' he whispered, but I wasn't listening.

'Oh, what's the point!' I cried, lifting my Detective Manksniff hat off my head and throwing it to the ground. 'My mum and dad don't love me . . . Irene is dead . . . and everybody in the whole wide school thinks I'm the Phantom Carton Crumpler!' I blubbered.

THUD.

I held my left hand up to my face and looked at it, wondering if I maybe did sleep-drink Anton's carton. 'I give up!' I wailed, and I pulled the straw out of my mouth and snapped it in half, which isn't easy, seeing as straws are bendy, not snappy.

SNAP!

The jumble sale

Nobody talked to me for the rest of the day after that, or for the whole of the night either, seeing as I was sitting in my room on my own, cuddling my crumpled carton of Irene like the loneliest loser since Great Uncle Desmond.

Then all of a non-sudden it was half past twelve on Saturday afternoon and I was in Mogden Hall, surrounded by eight million nattering grannies.

Everybody in the whole of Mogden was there, including Anton Mildew, who was standing behind his granny's stall giving me an evil stare.

My mum and dad wobbled up, pushing Desmond Loser the Second in his pram. 'Cheer up, Barry, it might never happen!' smiled my dad, but it was too late, it already had.

'Afternoon Kenneth,' I mumbled, because I'd stopped calling him Dad, seeing as I wasn't his number one son any more.

I peered up at my mum and sighed, remembering when she used to love me like she loved Desmond. 'Don't worry Maureen, I'll only be around for another ten years or so, then I'm comperleeterly out of your hair,' I said, a Tear of Barry Sadness squeezing its way out of my eyeball.

'Oh, Barry,' said my mum, but I wasn't listening. Mr Hodgepodge had plodded on to the stage and was setting up his coffin.

'Oops!' he chuckled, dropping his saw, and it clanged on to the floorboards. 'Not a problem!' he smiled, picking it up with his shaky hand and slicing through a rope, and the curtain fell behind him.

'Oooh goody! Someone's gonna get chopped in half!' grinned Bunky, who was standing behind his granny's stall, being a walking stick for Nancy.

'Ladies and gentlemen, I am The Great Hodgepodge and today I am going to chop my glamorous assistant in two!' warbled Hodge, starting his magic show, and Madame Harumpadunk hobbled on to the stage, dressed in her spangly gold leotard and yellow tutu.

She glanced over my way and gulped, as everybody in the whole of Mogden Hall apart from me started clapping their hands. I looked around at them all, enjoying their Saturday afternoons, and wondered if I had anything left to live for.

Madame Harumpadunk closed her eyes and crossed herself, did a shaky wave to the audience and hoiked one of her legs into Mr Hodgepodge's coffin box.

'I wish somebody would chop ME in half,' I muttered to myself. 'I bet everyone would LOVE to see that!' I said, and an idea popped out of my head into the bit of air where my hat used to be. 'Hang on a millikeels ... STOP THE SHOW!' I wailed, and the whole of Mogden Hall went quiet.

The end for Barry Loser

'Chop ME in half!' I shouted, walking up the little stairs to the stage, and I heard Gordon Smugly chuckle.

'Barry, get down from there!' wailed my mum, lifting Des out of his pram, and I peered at her the way I peer at my mum when I'm about to be sawed into two Barrys.

'Maureen, Maureen, Maureen,' I sighed.
'Nobody wants to watch Madame
Harumpadunk get chopped up . . .
not when they can see the Phantom
Carton Crumpler face certain
deathypoos!' I boomed, and Anton
nodded his head.

Phantom
Carton
Crumpler

Mr Hodgepodge loosened his bow tie
and sighed. 'It's very kind of you to
offer, Barry, but your gran is really
looking forward to this,' he said,
pointing at my granny, who was still
clambering into the coffin, looking like
she was about to cry.

'Th-that's right, B-barry, I-let your old gran get chopped in half!' she stuttered, her feathers shaking with fear.

I walked towards the coffin, wondering how I was going to walk once my legs had been sawed off. 'I'm sorry, Mr Hodgepodge, but I really must insistypoos,' I said.

my legs walking off without me

'Well, if you're sure,' trembled my granny, clambering back out of the box and giving me a scrapey spangle hug. 'Thank you, Barry Warry!' she whispered in my ear, and I giggled, but only because it tickled.

I looked at The Great Hodgepodge and raised my eyebrows, waiting for him to say yes, and he scratched his bum with the non-sawing side of his saw.

'You'll have to wear the costume, of course,' he sighed, hoping that would be enough to put me off, and I heard Bunky gasp.

'You don't have to do this, Barry!' he wailed from the audience, but I wasn't listening.

'Pass me the tutu,' I said.

Madame Barry

'Phwoot-phwoo!' wolf-whistled Sharonella as I walked back on stage from the dressing room, wearing Madame Harumpadunk's spangly gold leotard and yellow tutu.

'Look after little Des for me, Maureen,'
I blubbered to my mum, as I climbed
into the coffin and saluted the crowd,
looking around one more time before I
was chopped into two bits and put in a
bin out the back of Mogden Hall.

'BLURGLE! GOOGOO!' garbled Desmond,
his dummy popping out of his mouth,
and he pointed over at Bunky.

what's Des
spotted?

'Yes, that's right Des,' I said. 'Bunky'll be your new brother once I'm gone, won't you Bunky?' I warbled, and I glanced at Bunky, hoping he'd agree.

'GURGLE! DOODOO!' blurgled Des, doing a sucking noise with his mouth, and I opened my eyes again and peeked out of the coffin, mainly because I was getting a tiny bit scared and hoped someone might stop me going through with it.

don't want to be chopped in half

'WAA WAA!' shrieked Des, waggling his arm at his new brother, and I looked at Bunky properly. Something about him reminded me of Detective Manksniff all of a sudden.

It wasn't his voice, because he wasn't saying anything. It wasn't his hat, because he didn't have one on. And it wasn't his smile, because he wasn't smiling.

'What in the name of Great Uncle Desmond Loser is it?' I mumbled, then I gasped, realising what it was. Sticking out of Bunky's trouser pocket was a little straw with pink tear shapes dotted all over it.

STRAW CLOSE-UP!

Bunky's straw

'Stop the show!' I boomed, jumping out of the coffin, and The Great Hodgepodge ripped his bow tie off, throwing it on the floor all disappointed.

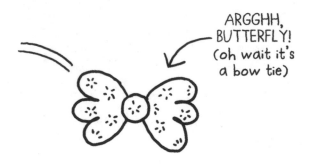

ARGGHH,
BUTTERFLY!
(oh wait it's
a bow tie)

I staggered towards Bunky, wondering how Desmond had recognised the Tears of Granny Laughter straw. Then I remembered him reaching out for the one on my carton of Irene that time when I was bouncing him on my mum's yoga ball.

The only question now was: what was Bunky doing with one sticking out of his pocket?

'B-bunky, w-where did you get that straw?' I stuttered.

Bunky tapped the straw, tucking it further down into his pocket. 'Er, umm, urggh . . .' he mumbled, looking around. Everyone had stopped staring at me and swivelled their eyeballs over to him.

His Daily Poo was still sticking out of his back pocket, and I whipped it out, staring at the photo of Anton's crumpled carton of Beryl on the front page.

'Just as I thought!' I boomed, pointing at the photo. 'There was no straw in Anton's carton after it'd been crumpled . . . Whoever drank Beryl must've stolen the straw as well!'

remember this bit too?

Tears of Granny Laughter

BERYL FLAVOUR

Photo by Gaspar Pink

'B-but this is the straw from the carton of Gertrude my sister bought me!' warbled Bunky, pincering it out of his pocket and sticking it between his lips, trying to look all innocent.

'What, the straw I snapped in half and Nancy threw in the bin?' I scoffed. 'I don't think so!' I said, snuffling my nostrils around the end of the straw.

'Anton,' I shouted, 'I think you'd better take a look at this.'

One last drop of Beryl

Anton wobbled over, giving me an evil stare. 'What do you want now, Beryl Murderer?' he said.

by the way, the real Beryl isn't dead

'Give this a snuffle,' I said, wafting the non-Bunky-spit end of the straw under his nose, and he breathed in, but not like he wanted to smell it, more because he needed to breathe to keep on being alive.

looking a bit worried

At first it was just a comperleeterly normal, everyday Anton Mildew breath. Then something happened to his face.

His eyes seemed to get bigger, and his hair went even more curly than usual.

ANTON FACE CHANGE!

'H-how in the why what when which why ...' he stuttered, snatching the straw out of my hands and holding it up to the window. 'B-beryl? 'Oh, my dear, sweet Beryl ...' he cried, dropping to his knees and beginning to sob.

Bunky's confession

I peered into Bunky's eyes the way I peer into them when I've just realised he's the one who drank Anton's carton of Tears of Granny Laughter.

'Don't hate me, Barry . . .' he begged, dropping his head so that he looked even more like a walking stick than before.

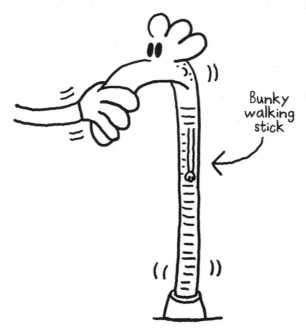

Bunky walking stick

'Oh Bunky, how COULD you?' said Nancy, taking off her glasses.

Bunky put his hand on my shoulder and I shrugged it off, not believing my best friend could have done this to me. 'I'm so sorry . . .' he cried, as I stood there in my spangly gold leotard and yellow tutu, waiting to hear his explanation.

'I came looking for you when you went for your poo, but you weren't in the classroom. Then I saw Anton's carton . . .' he said, not finishing his sentence.

the scene of the crime

'I thought you didn't even like Tears of Granny Laughter?' I said, not looking at him. My whole body had turned to jelly, except the sort of jelly that's too upset to wobble.

comperleeterly
still

'I was just really thirsty. I didn't think . . .' said Bunky, shrugging his shoulders, and I wondered what kind of idiot drinks a drink he doesn't even like drinking, just because he fancies a drink. Then I remembered this was Bunky we were talking about.

'I thought you were right-handed,'
I said.

'I am,' said Bunky, holding his right hand
up and looking at it like it wasn't his.
'I was picking my nose with this one
when I crumpled the carton,' he said,
and I laughed to myself, in an angry
sort of way.

bogie
picker

carton
crumpler

'That's when I put the straw in my
pocket,' he mumbled, and we both
peered down at Anton, who was lying
on the ground sobbing, still clutching his
Beryl straw.

'It was just so keel, with its little pink tears dotted all over it . . . and I liked chewing on it too,' said Bunky.

I thought about how much I liked chewing on my Tears of Granny Laughter straw, and sort of knew what Bunky meant.

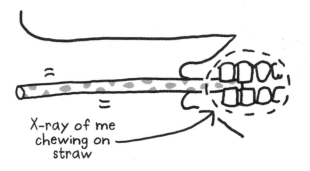

X-ray of me
chewing on
straw

'You let everyone think it was ME who stole it, though,' I said, turning round and staring into Bunky's eyes, and I remembered how he'd been acting all weird around me recently.

Bunky looked down at his feet, which were pointing towards each other all guiltily. 'I'm sozkeels, Barry,' he whispered. 'I was gonna say something, real-keely I was. Then Anton started screaming at you, and before I knew it . . .' he said, not finishing his sentence for the second time in three minutes.

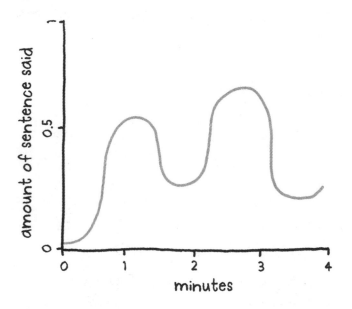

I'd always thought Bunky was the brave one out of us two, but looking at him now, I wasn't so sureypoos. After all, he hadn't even had the guts to admit he'd drunk a carton of granny tears, for crying out keel.

'PLEEEAAASE forgive me, Barry, I'll do ANYTHING,' squeaked Bunky, dropping to his knees, and I gave him one of my evil stares.

secretly enjoying being same height as him

You know when you're giving your best friend one of your evil stares, but all you can see is your best friend, standing there in front of you? That's what was happening now.

I thought about all the times I'd done something annoying to Bunky, and how he'd always forgiven me for it in the end. Then I looked down at my spangly gold leotard and yellow tutu. And that was when I came up with one of my brilliant and amazekeel ideas.

'ANYTHING, you say?' I said, starting to wriggle out of my glamorous assistant outfit.

Madame Bunky

'WAAAHHH!!!' screamed Bunky, as me and Anton carried him on to the stage. He was dressed in a spangly gold leotard and yellow tutu with feathers sticking out of his hair. 'HELLLP MEEE!!!' he wailed, as we lowered him into the coffin and slotted on the lid.

'Just a quick sliceypoos, then all is forgiven!' I said, patting the lid, and Mr Hodgepodge plodded over, putting his stick-on bow tie back on.

chopped-in-half Bunky

'Ladies and gentlemen, I am The Great Hodgepodge and today I am going to chop Madame Bunky in half!' he boomed, holding the saw up in his shaky hand.

I skipped down the steps from the stage and wandered over to my mum, who was holding Desmond Loser the Second, my dad with his arm round them both.

'I'm sorry I didn't believe you, Barry,' my mum whispered, as I glanced down at Granny Harumpadunk's stall and spotted the little china pig she'd slipped into her purse a few days before.

I picked it up and passed it to my mum. 'Sorry about breaking your other one into ten bits,' I said, and she grinned.

'BLURGLE! GOOGOO! BARRY!' gurgled Des, and my mum waggled her eyebrows.

'Barry! He said Barry!' she laughed, and my dad opened his arm out for me to join their cuddle.

I looked at my mum and dad, and my annoying baby brother, and wondered if they maybe weren't so bad after all. 'Eeve keelse!' I smiled, and I reached my arms around them all, which wasn't easy, because my dad's quite fat.

Actual real-life Tears of Granny Laughter

'And now for the cutting-in-half bit!' boomed The Great Hodgepodge, holding his saw up in the air with his shaky hand.

WAGGLE!

'HELLLPPP MEEEE, MUMMMMYYYY!!!'
screamed Bunky's voice from inside
the coffin, which is a pretty loserish
thing to scream, especially when you're
wearing a gold spangly leotard and
yellow tutu, with feathers in your hair.

Sharonella walked over to me, doing
a snortle. She cupped her hand round
her mouth and put it up to my ear.
'Thanks for not telling anyone about
the you-know-what, Bazza,' she
whispered, making my ear tickle.

'That's keel,' I smiled. 'You really shouldn't be stealing air-fresheners, though, Shazza,' I said, reminding myself of Detective Manksniff when he's teaching the baddy a lesson at the end of one of his shows.

The Barry Loser Show

Sharonella pointed the ends of her feet together, all guiltily. 'I know . . . I've been a bad Shazza,' she said, fluttering her eyelashes. 'That's why I'm gonna be the Phantom Air-Freshener Putter-Backerer from now on!' she beamed, and I patted her on the head and looked up at the stage.

'Er, what exactly is happening out there?' squeaked Bunky's voice from inside the coffin, and I chuckled to myself, feeling happy for the first time since sliced slices.

'Don't worry, Bunky, this won't hurt a bit!' warbled The Great Hodgepodge, and Anton started chuckling too. Then Nancy joined in, then Granny Harumpadunk, then her friend Ethel, then all the other grannies as well.

'Ooh, it is nice to have a little giggle, isn't it!' warbled Sharonella's gran, as a shiny, wet, teardrop-sized globule of liquid started to appear in the corner of her eye.

'I haven't laughed so much since I was this high!' cried Ethel, holding her hand up thirteen centimetres above her head, and a globule of liquid bubbled out of her eye too.

100% granny laughter tear

I Future-Ratboy-darted my eyes around Mogden Hall and counted seventeen more eyeball globules, all of them coming out of the corners of old grannies' eyes.

'Real-life Tears of Granny Laughter!' I cried, and Anton's eyes lit up.

get it?

'URGGH!' burped Darren Darrenofski, slurping on a can of Pineapple and Grapefruit Fronkle, and he wobbled towards the front door. 'I can't take any more of this!'

A 50p-sized puddle of real-life Tears of Granny Laughter had begun to spread out on the floor underneath Granny Harumpadunk and I gawped at it, remembering how much I'd wanted to try a carton.

'It was a bit of a stupid idea for a drink really, wasn't it,' I chuckled, imagining slurping up the puddle and feeling sick.

SLURRRPPP!

'It wasn't even that nice to be
honest with you Barry,' said Anton,
and I rolled my eyes to myself.

'What a comperleet and utter waste
of time!' I giggled, and I got ready to
watch my best friend in the whole
wide world amen get chopped in half.